For teachers everywhere—everyday superheroes.

American edition published in 2019 by Andersen Press USA,
an imprint of Andersen Press Ltd.
www.andersenpressusa.com

First published in Great Britain in 2019 by Andersen Press Ltd.,
20 Vauxhall Bridge Road, London SW1V 2SA.

Copyright © Robert Starling 2019

Distributed in the United States and Canada by
Lerner Publishing Group, Inc.
241 First Avenue North
Minneapolis, MN 55401 USA
For reading levels and more information, look up this title at www.lernerbooks.com.

Printed and bound in China by Toppan Leefung Ltd.

Library of Congress Cataloging-in-Publication Data Available

ISBN: 978-1-5415-5511-2
eBook ISBN: 978-1-5415-7794-7

1–TOPPAN–4/1/19

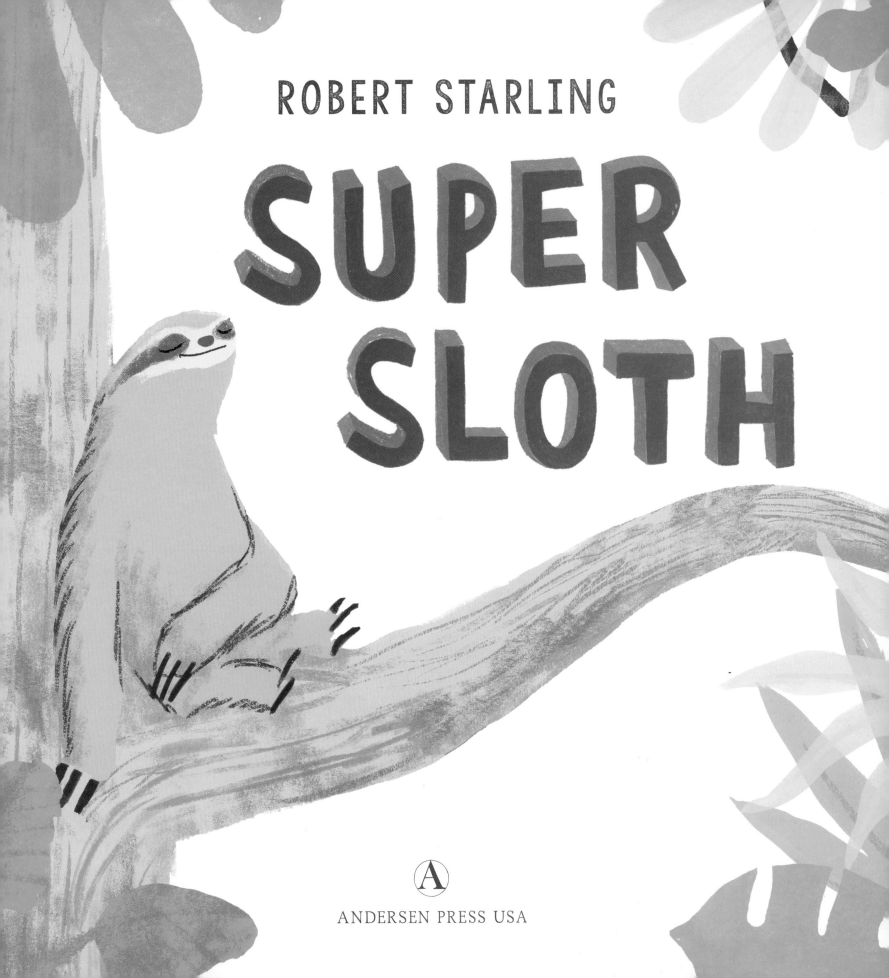

ROBERT STARLING

SUPER SLOTH

Ⓐ

ANDERSEN PRESS USA

In an ordinary jungle, up an ordinary tree, on an ordinary branch, there lived a very ordinary sloth.

He hung out in the same place every day and nothing much ever happened.

Until, one day, it did.

"What a strange leaf,"
thought Sloth.

It had little pictures drawn all over it, and the pictures told a story.

Sloth read
it all day,
all night,

and all the
next day too.

It was
amazing!

Wow! What if
Sloth could be
a superhero?

All he needed was a costume like the one in the pictures.

He already had a mask.

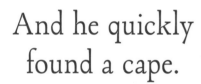

And he quickly found a cape.

Then he was ready to go and save the day! (Very slowly.)

It wasn't long before his super-sloth ears picked up a distant cry for help.

Help! Help! Someone's stealing my mangoes!

Sloth rushed over.

But by the time he got there,
it was too late.

"Oh, bother!"
said Sloth.

"It was that sneaky
Anteater!" cried Toucan.
"I don't have a single
mango left."

"Not to worry, Toucan," said Sloth. "I'll climb up
the highest tree, then I'll definitely spot the crook."

Eventually, something streaked across the forest floor.

"Now I'll catch that sneaky Anteater!" cried Sloth.

He stretched out his arms, spread his cape . . .

and launched himself from the tree.

"Bother," said Sloth. It didn't look this hard in the pictures.
"I guess I'm not meant to be a superhero after all."

The other animals
were just as glum.

"If we don't get our fruit back
from that greedy, guzzling
Anteater, we'll starve!"

"It's no good," said Bear. "We'll never get into his stronghold. He's got guards everywhere. Even his guards have guards!"

Bear had given Sloth an idea.
A sloth isn't fast.
A sloth can't fly.

But a sloth is very, very good
at moving slowly and looking
just like a tree.

RIGHT!

And this sloth
was also very,
very angry.

Little by little, hour by hour, Sloth crept closer and closer . . .

Not the other animals,

not the guards,

. . . to Anteater's hideaway.

And nobody noticed him.

not the guards of the guards.

Not even Anteater.

And so it was that slow old Sloth with his mossy fur . . .

He got right up next to Anteater . . .

Terrified, Anteater and
all his guards ran away.

Sloth had done it—
he'd gotten everyone's
mangoes back!

From that day on, wherever there were animals in trouble,

whenever danger had to be faced,

brave Super Sloth would be there.

Eventually.

Sloth Facts

Their fur is actually a mini ecosystem with algae and fungus growing on it and moths living in it!

Sloths spend most of their lives high up in the trees of the rainforest, coming down once a week to defecate*.

*That means poo.

Say hello to the brown-throated **sloth** (Bradypus variegatus).

They are found in South America.

They are part of the **three-toed sloth family** (because they have three claws on each hand for climbing).